Did you know
That Bumble-Ardy missed
Eight birthdays in a row?

MAURICE SENDAK

BUMBLE-ARDY

MICHAEL DI CAPUA BOOKS • HARPER COLLINS PUBLISHERS

Copyright © 2011 by Maurice Sendak • Moral rights asserted

Designed by David Saylor and Charles Kreloff • Thanks to Dorothy Pietrewicz

ISBN 978-0-00-744738-1 • Printed in the USA • 8 7 6 5 4 3 2 1

PROLOGUE

Bumble-Ardy had no party when he turned one.

(His immediate family frowned on fun.)

So two three and four were on purpose forgot

And five six seven just simply were not!

But when Bumble was eight

(Oh, pig-knuckled fate!)

His immediate family gorged and gained weight.

And got ate.

So Adeline, that aunt divine,

Adopted Bumble when he was nine.

Now, ain't that fine?

Bumble-Ardy had a party when he was nine.

Which isn't bad.

In fact, it's fine.

And just in time he asked some grubby swine

To come for birthday cake and brine at ten past nine.

Which isn't bad.

In fact, it's fine.

Except his aunt, sweet Adeline,
Who left the house at one past nine
To go to work at Smith & Klein,

Just hated swine to drink her brine—
Not even on a day so fine
As Bumble's birthday number nine.

So he simply didn't tell her.

At nine past nine the piggy swine
Broke down the door and guzzled brine

And hogged sweet cakes and oinked loud grunts
And pulled all kinds of dirty stunts.

Except just then dear Adeline,
Who finished work at half past nine
And hurried home so she could dine

With Bumble on his birthday nine
And found a mob of swilling swine,
Began to shriek and shake and whine.

So Adeline, that aunt divine,
Took in her Bumble valentine
And kissed him nine times over nine.

Now, ain't that fine?